BEWARE,
THIS HOUSE IS
HAUNTED !

Other Apple Paperbacks
you will want to read:

The Ghosts of Hungryhouse Lane
by Sam McBratney

The Hairy Horror Trick
by Scott Corbett

The Ghosts Who Went to School
by Judith Spearing

The Ghostmobile
by Kathy Kennedy Tapp

BEWARE, THIS HOUSE IS HAUNTED!

Lance Salway

AN
APPLE
PAPERBACK

SCHOLASTIC INC.
New York Toronto London Auckland Sydney

ISBN 0-590-43390-3

12 11 10 9 8 7 6 5 4 3 2 1   0 1 2 3 4 5/9

Printed in the U.S.A.   40

First Scholastic printing, November 1990

BEWARE, THIS HOUSE IS HAUNTED !

1

The note came from nowhere. At least, that's how it seemed to Jessica when she found it in the kitchen on that rainy August morning. The note hadn't been there at breakfast time because she would have noticed it at once. She felt quite sure of that. But now, half an hour later, there it was: a tattered piece of paper pinned to the bulletin board next to the map of local beauty spots, and right on top of the list of things to do if the water heater started to make exploding noises.

Jessica stared at the note for a moment or two. She couldn't make out the words at first, because the paper was creased and the writing was scratchy and uneven. But it didn't take her long to work out that it read:

BEWARE,
THIS HOUSE
IS HAUNTED!

"How stupid!" Jessica said out loud. "As if there could possibly be ghosts in a place like *this*." But she looked quickly round the kitchen just to make sure.

"How stupid!" she said again. She reached up to pull the note from the board and then thought better of it. No, it would be best to leave it where it was. She'd pretend that she hadn't seen the note at all. It was nothing to do with her. And anyway, the others needn't think that she'd be impressed by a childish joke like *that*.

She turned towards the fridge and was just about to open the door when she was aware of a sudden movement behind her, as though someone had come into the room. She whirled round but there was no one to be seen. The kitchen was empty.

Jessica shivered. She could have sworn that someone else had been there, walking towards her. And the room seemed suddenly colder . . . Then she laughed out loud and told herself not to be such an idiot. She was imagining things, that's all. All because of the note. Just because that stupid note on the board had said that the house was haunted didn't mean that it really *was*. Anyway, it wasn't that sort of house. No ghost worthy of the name would be seen dead in a neat, white-washed holiday cottage in Cornwall, with hy-

2

drangeas by the front door and a colour telly in the sitting room; they much preferred dilapidated, ivy-covered mansions with ruined turrets and stained-glass windows and bats in the attics. No, *this* house wasn't haunted. Someone else had written the note. Her sister Lizzie, perhaps. Or one of the Monsters, more likely.

She walked across to the board to take another look at the note. It was still there, with its silly message scrawled in spidery capitals. And then, as she stepped closer, Jessica could see that something else was scribbled at the bottom of the piece of paper, words that she hadn't noticed before:

IGNORE THIS AT YOUR PERIL.
YOU HAVE BEEN WARNED!

Jessica gave a sharp nervous laugh. How ridiculous! How utterly pathetic! Did they really expect her to be taken in by that? And yet, at the same time, she felt suddenly uneasy. She could have sworn that nothing else had been written on the piece of paper when she saw it first. The message had simply read: BEWARE, THIS HOUSE IS HAUNTED! and that was all. There had been nothing else on the paper, she felt sure of that. There had been nothing else there at all.

"Oh, pull yourself together, Jessica," she told

herself firmly. "You're imagining things. It's all this rain. It's sending you bananas. Forget about that stupid note. It's only Lizzie trying to be funny, as usual." And she turned away and walked quickly out of the room, slamming the door behind her.

She found Lizzie in the sitting room, slumped in an armchair and gazing glumly at the television set. On the screen, two cowboys were busily riding across a rocky hillside.

Jessica paused for a moment to watch and then said, "That fair one gets shot. In a minute they're going to ride into a gorge and a lot of other men will be waiting for them. Hiding. Then there's a big gunfight and the fair one gets shot."

"Thanks *very* much," Lizzie said indignantly. "You've spoiled it all now. Anyway, how do you know?"

"I've seen it before," Jessica said, and then added unkindly, "It's a rotten film, anyway." She crossed to the window and stared out. Rain was rattling spitefully on the glass, and the garden outside was hidden in a dense grey mist. Mrs Pengelly, who owned the cottage, had told them that you could see the cove and the cliffs and the sea from the windows but it had rained continuously ever since their arrival three days ago and there'd been no sign of any view at all. They might just as well have been on Mars.

Jessica sighed. The sound of gunfire from the television told her that the cowboys had at last ridden into the ambush.

"You're right," Lizzie said after a while. "As usual. The fair one *did* get shot."

Jessica turned to look at her. "Where are all the others?" she asked.

Lizzie frowned. "What others! Oh, I see what you mean. Mum and Andrew have gone down to the village to buy food and stuff. And she said something about going for a walk on the beach afterwards."

"In this weather? They must be mad."

"They *are* mad," Lizzie said. "If that's what getting married does to you then you can keep it."

Jessica nodded. Her mother and Andrew had been married now for over six months but they still carried on as if they were six-year-olds. It was sickening. You'd think that they'd have known better at their age. Her mother was at least thirty-five and Andrew was even older.

"And what about the Monsters?" Jessica asked. "Where are *they*?"

Lizzie lowered her voice. "The big one's gone

5

out somewhere. I think he said something about exploring the cove. With any luck he'll drown."

"And the one with glasses?"

"He's in his room, I think . . . reading." Lizzie stared at the television screen for a moment or two without really seeing it. Then she looked up at Jessica and said imploringly, "Oh, *why* did the Monsters have to come? They're so awful. I hate them. It's going to be the worst holiday ever."

"I know," Jessica said. "I hate them too. But there's nothing we can do about it, is there? We're stuck with them, whether we like it or not."

"Can't you do something to get rid of them?" Lizzie asked plaintively. "You always know what to do. You always have such good ideas."

Jessica sighed again. "Not this time I don't," she muttered. "Anyway, I'm sick of being expected to come up with the answer to every problem." She turned back to the window and gazed miserably out into the rain. Lizzie was right. It *was* going to be the worst holiday ever.

It had seemed such a good idea when her mother had first told them about it, all those weeks before. "We've decided to go to Cornwall for our holiday this year," she'd said brightly. "Andrew's heard about a marvellous cottage at a place called Ottercombe. It'll be perfect for the four of us. Our first holiday together as a family." And she'd beamed at them so happily that Jessica and Lizzie had been forced to agree that yes, it sounded lovely. Secretly, though, they were both disappointed. They'd been hoping for a holiday abroad, in Spain perhaps, or Greece. Their mother and Andrew had gone to Venice for their honeymoon and it seemed only fair that they should now take Jessica and Lizzie abroad too. But their mother had only laughed when they suggested this. "We're not made of money, you know," she'd said. "No, we'll have a lovely time in Cornwall. Just you wait and see."

But they hadn't bargained for the weather. Or the Monsters.

The Monsters were called Martin and Gareth, and they were Andrew's children from his first marriage to a woman called Angela. Martin was twelve, the same age as Jessica, and Gareth, like Lizzie, was a year younger. Jessica and Lizzie had never met them because the boys lived in Chelmsford with their mother. All that changed, however, a fortnight before they were due to leave for Cornwall.

One evening at supper, Jessica's mother had smiled at them nervously and said, "You'll never guess what's happened!"

Jessica and Lizzie had stared at her stonily, expecting the worst. They were not disappointed.

7

"Angela's going to America for a month," their mother went on cheerfully. "It's to do with her work — a conference of some kind, I think. Anyway, she can't take Martin and Gareth with her so — "

"So they're coming with us to Cornwall," Jessica finished dully. "And ruining our holiday into the bargain."

"Now don't be silly, Jessica." Her mother had stopped smiling now. "We're all going to have a lovely time. One big family together. And I'm relying on you both to make the boys feel at home."

It was Lizzie who started calling the boys "the Monsters." This was partly because of their surname, which was Monson, but mainly because she and Jessica had taken a violent dislike to them before they had even met. After all, they were sure to be awful, weren't they, these ghastly boys who'd spoiled their holiday before it had even begun?

As it turned out, it was obvious that Martin and Gareth hated the idea of going on holiday with the girls just as much as they did, and so the journey down to Cornwall in Andrew's Volvo took place in stony silence. Their parents chattered happily for a while in an attempt to lighten the atmosphere but even they gave up after a time and sat in

8

silence for the rest of the journey. The boys didn't *look* like Monsters — they both had fair curly hair and freckles, like their father — but by the time Jessica had thawed enough to give Martin a wintry smile when he sullenly offered her one of his liquorice allsorts, Gareth spoiled it all by being sick all over Lizzie. When they arrived at the cottage, they were all feeling tired and bad-tempered, and the fact that it started to rain as soon as they stepped out of the car, and hadn't stopped since, only made everything worse.

Now, as she stared miserably out into the rain, Jessica wished yet again that the holiday was over and that they could all go home. It wouldn't have been so bad if the sun was shining. At least they'd have been able to go outside, and get away from the Monsters. Being cooped up together in the cottage, day after dismal day, only made everyone bad-tempered.

It was then that she remembered the note on the board, the childish note about the house being haunted. She turned to look at Lizzie, who was once more absorbed in the action on the television screen.

"I suppose you think that note on the board is a big joke," Jessica said, trying to sound as casual as possible.

Lizzie looked up at her blankly. "What note?"

"The note on the board in the kitchen. The one with the warning."

"I don't know what you're talking about," Lizzie said impatiently, and turned back to the film.

Jessica looked at her in silence for a moment or two. She could always tell when Lizzie was telling the truth. So, one of those ghastly boys must have written the note. The one with glasses, probably. Gareth. The other Monster was probably too stupid. He was probably too thick even to write his own name, let alone a warning about ghosts.

She walked quickly out of the room and back into the kitchen. The note was still there, pinned to the board alongside the list of local pubs and the bus timetables and the note about putting out the dustbin on Friday mornings. Jessica reached up and pulled the piece of paper from the drawing pin that held it to the board. She stared at the note for a moment, and then crumpled it up and flung it into the waste bin by the sink.

That would show them. That would show them that she wasn't impressed by their pathetic attempts at humour. So the house was haunted, was it? Really, how childish could you get? And she stalked out of the kitchen and went to watch the rest of the film with Lizzie.

2

Jessica didn't sleep very well that night. She lay awake for hours, or so it seemed, listening to the rain pattering on the window and to Lizzie's level breathing in the next bed. Every time she started to feel drowsy, a sudden creak in the ceiling or gust of wind outside would jolt her wide awake again. After a while, she began to wonder if the house really *was* haunted. Perhaps the noise outside wasn't just wind blowing round the house but a ghost howling to come in. Perhaps those creaks in the ceiling weren't just the ordinary sounds you hear in an old cottage but ghostly footsteps walking overhead. Perhaps there really *was* a ghost upstairs, in the attic, waiting to creep out as soon as she fell asleep.

She must have dozed off after a while because the next time she opened her eyes the bedroom was flooded with daylight and Lizzie was shaking her and saying, "Come on, Jess, breakfast's ready. You've overslept."

Jessica groaned and said grumpily, "Well, so what? I'm on holiday, aren't I?" before turning over and burying her face in the pillow.

By the time she came downstairs and joined the others in the kitchen, they had finished their cereal and had started on toast and marmalade.

"Well, look who's here!" Andrew said cheerfully when she appeared. "Glad you could join us at last, Jess."

Jessica shot him an icy glare and sat down at the table.

"You could at least say good morning," her mother said. "There's no need to be rude as well as late."

"Good morning," Jessica mumbled sullenly, and reached for the cereal packet.

"You might try and sound as if you meant it," her mother sniffed. "Still, I can't say there's much good about the morning. I don't think this rain is *ever* going to stop."

What a stupid thing to say, Jessica thought. Of course the rain's going to stop. *One* day. Next week, maybe. Or next year. Then, "There's none left!" she shouted indignantly.

"None what left?" Andrew asked.

"Ricey-Pops," Jessica said. "All the Ricey-Pops have gone."

"Well, have something else, then," her mother said wearily. "Corn flakes, muesli . . ."

"You know I only like Ricey-Pops," Jessica persisted. "Who finished them?"

"I did," said Martin. He grinned at her mockingly.

"Who said *you* could have them?" Jessica shouted. "The Ricey-Pops are *mine*! You've no right to — "

"For heaven's sake!" her mother said irritably. "What does it matter? We'll get some more today. *Two* packets, if you like."

"Ten," put in Andrew.

"I want some *now*," Jessica said. "Anyway, that's not the point. They were mine and *he* took them."

Jessica's mother banged her fist on the table.

"They were not yours, Jessica. They were *ours*. Martin has just as much right to them as you have," she said.

"If you'd been up in time, *you* could have had them instead," Gareth said, and Lizzie giggled.

Jessica shot Gareth a glare that could have shattered glass. "Drop dead, donkey face," she said.

"Pick on someone your own size!" Martin said

angrily. "Leave my brother alone."

"Oh get lost, you stupid — "

"Jessica, that's *enough*!" her mother shouted.

There was an uncomfortable silence for a moment or two, and then Andrew said brightly, "Well then, what shall we all do today?"

"Go back to London," Jessica muttered.

Andrew wisely decided to ignore her. "I think we should head for St Ives. It's an interesting old town and there's a fishing harbour and beaches to visit if the rain stops."

"And if it doesn't?" Jessica's mother asked sourly.

"Well, there are art galleries to look round. And plenty of shops, of course."

"Oh good," Lizzie said, brightening. She loved going into shops even though she could rarely afford to buy anything.

Andrew pushed back his chair and stood up. "Well, we'll just nip down to the village for more Ricey-Pops and things while you kids do the washing up."

"Us?" said Jessica. "Why us?"

"Because it's your job," Andrew said. "And because *I* say so. Okay?"

"Well, *I'm* not doing it," she said.

"Nor me," Martin added. "And neither is my brother."

Jessica's mother glared at them. "I don't care which of you does it as long as it's done by the time we get back. Understand?" She stood up then and walked angrily out of the kitchen, closely followed by Andrew.

There was silence for a while after that, broken only by the sounds of rain on the window and Jessica noisily munching toast and marmalade.

At last Lizzie said, "Well, I suppose we'd better do the washing up like he said."

"I don't see why." Jessica pointed at Martin with her piece of toast and added, "Let *him* do it. He's the one who ate my Ricey-Pops."

"They weren't *yours*," Martin said angrily. "They were everyone's. And anyway, what does — "

"We could take it in turns," Gareth said.

The others stared at him. "Take what in turns?" Jessica asked. "Eating Ricey-Pops?"

"Don't be stupid," Gareth said scornfully. "The washing up. You do it today and someone else can do it tomorrow. And someone else the day after that."

"I'm not doing it today," Jessica said quickly.

"Nor me," Martin added.

"Gareth's right," said Lizzie. "It's a good idea. We'll take it in turns."

"We could write a list," Gareth suggested. "We

15

could put down who does washing up on which day."

"But who's going to do it first?" Martin asked. "I'm not."

"Nor me," Jessica muttered. "Anyway, I think the boys should do it. *Every* day."

Gareth took no notice. "We'll put the names down in alphabetical order. That's the fairest way." He got up and crossed to the dresser for a pad and pencil.

"Gareth, Jessica, Lizzie, Martin," Lizzie said. "Those are our names in alphabetical order. So it's your turn first, Gareth."

He looked at her. "Isn't Lizzie short for Elizabeth?"

"Yes, of course it is. *No*. No, it isn't."

"Yes, it is," Jessica said nastily. "Lizzie *is* short for Elizabeth. So it's *your* turn first, Lizzie. Serves you right for being so clever."

"But no one ever calls me Elizabeth," Lizzie protested.

"Doesn't matter," Martin said firmly. "It's your real name so you come first on the list. It's your turn this morning. Give me the list when you've finished, Gareth. I'll stick it up on the board." The others watched in silence as Gareth wrote down their names with a day of the week beside each. Then Martin took the list across to the bulletin board and pinned it neatly in the top left-hand corner. He was just about to turn away when he caught sight of a scrap of paper that was pinned towards the bottom of the board.

"Oh, very clever, I must say!" he sneered.

"What is?" Jessica snapped. She got up from her chair and crossed to join him.

"This note," Martin said. "I suppose *you're* the bird-brain who wrote it."

The piece of paper was covered with familiar spindly capitals which read:

THIS HOUSE IS DEFINITELY HAUNTED.
I AM NOT JOKING.
GET OUT BEFORE IT'S TOO LATE.

Jessica felt suddenly cold, and she shivered. "I didn't write it," she said. "It wasn't me."

"Then who did?" Martin asked.

"You, I expect," she said. "And I bet you wrote the note yesterday, too."

"What note yesterday? I didn't see a note yesterday." Martin seemed genuinely puzzled and Jessica had an uncomfortable feeling that he was telling the truth.

"There was a message like this on the board yesterday," she muttered. "In the same writing. It said that this house is haunted."

17

There was silence for a moment and then Lizzie said nervously, "It's not true, is it? This house isn't really haunted? There aren't really any ghosts here, are there?"

Jessica turned to look at her. Lizzie's face was pale and her dark eyes were wide with alarm. "No, of course not," Jessica said. "How could there be? There's no such things as ghosts. They don't exist."

"Jess is right," Martin said. "Don't worry, Lizzie. This house isn't haunted. There aren't any ghosts here at — "

There was a sudden loud crash. Jessica whirled round and saw that a large plate had fallen from one of the dresser shelves and smashed to pieces on the floor.

The children stared at the broken plate open-mouthed for a moment, and then Gareth stammered, "How — how did *that* happen?"

"It was — it was a draught or something, I expect," Martin said uneasily. "Just one of those things."

"But why didn't any of the other plates fall off too?" Lizzie's voice was trembling. "A ghost did it. I know a ghost did it. This house *is* haunted, it's — "

"Oh, don't be so feeble!" Jessica snapped. "Ghosts only happen in books." And then she gave a sudden gasp as the kitchen door swung violently open and then, almost immediately, slammed shut again with an ear-splitting bang.

"You see?" said Martin. "It's just a draught. Old houses like this are full of draughts. That's why the door opened. And that's why the plate fell and broke. That's what happened . . ." His voice tailed off and he looked defiantly at Jessica.

"That door was firmly shut," Jessica said. "I don't see how a draught could have opened it."

"Well, it did," Martin said. "If it wasn't a draught, then how did it happen? Unless," he went on scornfully, "you think that it opened all by itself."

Jessica glared at him. She opened her mouth to say something rude in reply and then changed her mind and shut it again.

"I'm going to get ready," she muttered, and started to walk to the door. Then she stopped dead as the door began to open again. She heard Lizzie let out a yelp of fear behind her, and felt her own heart thumping in her chest as the door opened wider. And then she laughed with relief when she saw that Andrew was standing in the doorway, clutching two large packets of Ricey-Pops.

"What's the matter, Jess?" he said. "You look as if you've just seen a ghost." Then he turned to the others. "Come on, you lot. We can get going as soon as you've done that washing up. It looks as though the rain might be stopping at last."

He was right. The rain *did* stop, but only long enough for them to drive to St Ives. As soon as they got out of the car, the skies opened once again and the pale sunshine was replaced by chill grey rain. By the time they returned to the cottage that afternoon, everyone was feeling damp and depressed.

"Maybe Jess was right," Andrew said as he unlocked the front door. "Maybe we *should* go back to London."

Jessica looked up hopefully at this but her face fell when her mother said, "Don't be stupid. The weather might change at any moment. Anyway, *I'm* enjoying myself." But she didn't look as if she was having a good time.

As soon as she got inside, Jessica headed straight for the kitchen and it was there that Martin found her, staring at another note on the board. This time the message read:

THIS IS YOUR FINAL WARNING.
THIS HOUSE IS HAUNTED
AND YOU ARE NOT WELCOME HERE.
LEAVE NOW IF YOU VALUE YOUR LIFE.

Martin muttered something under his breath and ripped the note from the board. Then he crumpled it up and put it in his pocket. "We'd better not let the others see this," he said. "Lizzie's frightened enough as it is." He stared at Jessica with his mocking blue eyes. "I suppose you think you're being clever."

She gaped at him. "What do you mean?"

"Writing these stupid notes, that's what I mean."

"I didn't write them," she said. "It wasn't me. Anyway, what chance have I had to write *anything*? I've been out all day. We both have."

Martin's face fell. "But who else can it be?" he said. "*Someone* must be writing them. If it wasn't one of us, then it must be — "

"Mrs Pengelly," Jessica said quickly. "I bet it's her. I bet she sneaks in here while we're out and leaves the notes. She wants to get rid of us. She's trying to frighten us away."

"But why?"

"I don't know. But who else could it be?" She paused, and then, when he didn't answer, she went on: "You don't *really* think this house is haunted, do you? You don't *really* think a ghost is leaving messages for us?"

"No, of course not," Martin said uneasily. "Of course I don't. All the same I — "

Jessica's mother came into the kitchen just then and they started to talk about something else. She looked at them curiously and said, "I'm glad to see that you two are getting on a bit better now."

"We aren't," Jessica said sharply. "We're having a conversation, that's all."

"Good," her mother said. "That's a start, anyway. Now then, what do you feel like having for tea?"

That night Jessica woke up with a start. She lay still for a moment, wondering what had woken her. And then, all at once, she knew. There was someone in the room. She couldn't see anything in the darkness, but she knew that someone else was there; she could feel that someone, or something, was watching her.

She sat up in bed and stared into the dark. "Who are you?" she breathed. "Who are you? What do you want?"

There was a sudden rustling noise beside her, and then Jessica heard laughter, shrill terrifying laughter that seemed to come from the foot of her bed. And then, as quickly as it had come, the presence was gone. Jessica was alone again, and the only sounds she could hear were Lizzie's breathing and the thumping of her own heart.

She sank back on to the pillows, her mind racing. It was her imagination, surely. She'd only imagined that someone else was in the room. It was all the fault of those notes and that stupid talk about ghosts. She'd only imagined it. She'd been dreaming. The laughter she'd heard was probably Martin or one of the others. But it had seemed so close . . .

When Jessica fell asleep at last, she dreamed that she was being chased down a long dark passage by a grinning white skeleton with eyes like fire.

3

J essica was late for breakfast the next morning so she didn't have a chance to look at the bulletin board to see if another message had appeared during the night. By the time she arrived in the kitchen, the others were all sitting at the table, busily eating boiled eggs and toast.

"Ah, there you are," her mother said. "This is getting to be a habit, I see."

"What is?" Jessica asked as she sat down.

"Being late for breakfast."

Jessica didn't say anything. Instead she turned to Martin and raised her eyebrows questioningly. He looked puzzled for a moment and then, when she jerked her head in the direction of the bulletin board, he nodded solemnly and patted his jeans pocket. Jessica pulled a face, and then turned away to find Andrew smiling at her across the table.

24

"What's going on?" he asked. "Is this some new kind of sign language?"

"You *could* say that," Martin said guardedly.

"I suppose it's asking too much to be let in on the secret," his father said, and then, when Martin nodded briskly, added, "I thought so."

"I suppose your lateness, Jess, is the result of all the noise last night," her mother said frostily.

Jessica stared at her in surprise. "What — what noise?" she stammered.

Her mother looked impatient. "You know perfectly well what noise. All that laughing. No wonder you overslept this morning."

Jessica shot a glance at Martin but he was staring down at his plate and didn't look at her. Had he heard laughter in the night too? Surely not — it had only been her imagination. But if her mother had heard something as well . . .

"You might show a little consideration for the rest of us in the future," her mother said.

"Yes — er — sorry," Jessica mumbled, and took a large mouthful of toast so that she couldn't say anything else without being bad-mannered.

The rest of the meal passed in silence. At last, Andrew stood up and said, "Well, we'll leave you to clear away. Whose turn is it today?"

"Mine, worse luck," said Gareth.

"Never mind," his father said. "We're going to pop down to the beach now for a quick walk. We can decide how we're going to spend the day when we get back. I may be wrong, but it looks as though the rain is going to hold off for once."

"And pigs might fly," Jessica's mother said gloomily as she followed Andrew out of the kitchen.

When their parents had gone, Gareth started to clear the table with Lizzie's help. Jessica watched them in silence for a moment and then she turned to Martin and said, "Did *you* hear anything last night?" He nodded, and she went on, "I did too. I heard someone laughing. And there was something in my room. I thought I was only dreaming but I couldn't have been if you heard it too. And Mum." She paused. "Who was making the noise? You don't think it could have been . . ." She stopped, not wanting to say the word out loud.

"A ghost?" Martin's voice was sharp with tension. "I don't know. Maybe it was. There was another note on the board this morning. I grabbed it before my dad could see it." He produced a crumpled piece of paper from his pocket and unfolded it carefully before passing it to Jessica. She peered down at the creased paper, not wanting to believe her eyes. This time the message read:

LAST NIGHT WAS JUST THE
BEGINNING. THIS IS DEFINITELY
YOUR LAST WARNING.
IF YOU DON'T LEAVE NOW,
IT WILL BE THE WORSE FOR YOU.

Jessica stared at the note for a moment or two and then tore it angrily into very small pieces.

"I don't know who's writing these messages," she said. "Perhaps it *is* a ghost. Or maybe it's someone else. One of us, even. I don't know. But I've had enough. I'll show whoever it is that they're not the only ones who can leave notes. Give me something to write on, Martin."

He crossed to the dresser for the pad and a Biro and passed them to her. She thought hard for a moment and then wrote, in large clear capital letters:

YOU CAN'T FRIGHTEN US.
WE ARE STAYING PUT.
IF YOU REALLY ARE A GHOST
THEN PROVE IT.
SHOW YOURSELF IF YOU DARE.

Jessica got up and pinned the note right in the centre of the bulletin board. "There," she said. "Let's see what happens now."

27

Martin looked at her nervously. "Are you sure this is a good idea? What if it's — if it's . . ." his voice tailed off.

Jessica looked at him scornfully. "You're not scared, are you?"

"Of course not. I just wondered if it was the right thing to do, that's all."

By now the others had joined them at the board.

"You told me there weren't any ghosts here," Lizzie said nervously. "You said that this house isn't haunted."

"I know I did," Jessica said. "And I still say there aren't any ghosts." She paused, hoping that she sounded braver than she felt. She wasn't so sure any more, not after last night. There *had* been someone in her room, and she *did* hear someone laughing. Perhaps the house really *was* haunted . . . "I just want to make certain, one way or the other," she said. "If nothing happens now, then we'll know there isn't a ghost."

"What must we do?" Gareth asked. His eyes were wide and anxious behind his glasses.

"Just sit here and wait," Jessica said, sinking onto a chair. "We'll give it five minutes. If nothing happens . . ." She paused, and then raised her voice defiantly and looked up at the ceiling. "If nothing happens we'll know that this house *isn't* haunted."

The others joined her at the table, and they sat in silence, waiting and listening. There was no sound at first, just the distant murmur of the sea and the ticking of a clock somewhere in the cottage. And then, without warning, the door was flung open and a gust of chill air swept into the kitchen.

Lizzie gave a little sob and Jessica reached for her hand. "It's all right," she whispered.

"It's just a draught," Martin said shakily. "Like yesterday, when the plate fell down. It's nothing to worry about . . ."

Jessica stared at the door, waiting for someone or something to appear. And then, as she watched, the air seemed to shimmer in front of her, like a mirage, and the outline of a human figure appeared. She heard a moan from one of the others and she knew that they had noticed the shape too. Then, slowly but surely, the form became more distinct, the trembling shape grew more solid, and she could soon make out pale arms, legs covered in something that was navy blue, and two sharp, glittering eyes behind a pair of spectacles.

Jessica hadn't given much thought to what the ghost might look like. She'd half expected it to be a shapeless figure draped in a sheet, like a ghost in a comic, or a woman with her head tucked underneath her arm, or a skeleton with fiery eyes, like the ghost in her dream. What she had *not* expected was a girl of about her own age, with a pale, pointed face and dark, shiny eyes framed by wire-rimmed spectacles. She was wearing a creased and stained black gym-slip and wrinkled, blue woollen stockings, and her straight hair was cut in a short untidy bob. She looked like the picture of a girl in an old-fashioned school story.

"Well, here I am!" the girl said. "You wanted to see me and here I am!"

No one said anything. Jessica stared at the girl, unable to believe her eyes.

"Cat got your tongues, has it?" The girl's voice was light and mocking. "Well, it's not surprising, really. Under the circumstances."

Lizzie surprised them all by being the first to say something. "Are you — are you a g-ghost?" she quavered. "Are you *really* a ghost?"

The girl stared at her for a moment and then burst out laughing. It was the same laugh that Jessica had heard in her room the night before.

"Yes," she said at last. "I'm a ghost, all right." She took a step towards Lizzie. "Here, you can touch me, if you like. You'll soon see if I'm real or not."

Lizzie shrank back and the girl laughed again. "I told you this house was haunted but you wouldn't believe me." Her voice was harsher now and her eyes gleamed like black pebbles. "Perhaps you'll believe me now."

Jessica gulped and said hoarsely, "I believe you. Was that you in my room last night?"

The girl grinned at her. "Yes, that was me. As I said, that was only the beginning. You've got to leave here. All of you. This is *my* house and I don't want anyone else here."

"And if we don't go?" Martin asked.

"If you don't, then — then things will get much worse, believe me. Dreadful things will happen."

"What sort of things?"

The ghost waved a vague hand. "All sorts of things. You don't think I'm going to tell you what they are in advance, do you? I'm not stupid."

"You're not as frightening as I expected," Lizzie said. "What's your name?"

The girl seemed taken aback by this question. She paused, and then said, "Beryl. Beryl Bowditch. *Not* that it's any of your business."

"*My* name's Elizabeth Harding," Lizzie said.

"I know," said Beryl. "I know all about you. All of you." For a moment it looked as though she was about to smile but she stopped herself just in time and scowled instead. "I want you to leave. At once. Now. I've warned you. Things will get much worse if you don't go."

"I don't believe you," Jessica said. How could anyone be afraid of a ghost who looked like a twelve-year-old schoolgirl from an old-fashioned book? "We're not frightened of *you*," she went on boldly. "It'll take more than a pipsqueak like you to scare *us*. And we're not leaving this cottage. Not until our fortnight's up, anyway."

Beryl glared at Jessica, her eyes bright with dislike. Her thin mouth was twisted into a sneer.

"We'll see about that," she hissed. "We'll see about *that*!"

And then, as they watched in amazement, she began to fade and dissolve until her body was just a vague outline, a shimmering shape that drifted in the air for a moment before vanishing completely.

There was silence for a long while after Beryl had gone. Then Gareth said, "Wow! How about *that*!"

"I don't believe it," Martin said, shaking his head. "I just don't believe it."

"It's true," Jessica said. "It really happened. But I'll tell you one thing. She's not going to get rid of us *that* easily. Oh no. No ghost called Beryl is going to get the better of *me*!"

4

No one said anything for a long time after that. Jessica crossed to the sink and started on the washing up. It wasn't her turn but she felt that she had to do something, *anything*, to try to forget what had happened.

Gareth picked up a tea towel and came to join her. "You shouldn't be doing that," he said. "It's my turn."

"Oh, I don't mind," Jessica mumbled.

He didn't mention the ghost and so she didn't say anything more about it either. It was almost as if none of them now wanted to admit that they had actually seen it. Perhaps they hadn't, Jessica thought. Perhaps they had all imagined it. But how could four people imagine the same thing at the same time? Or perhaps it was just a dream. Yes, that was it. Any minute now she'd wake up and find that she was in bed and none of it had really happened. There was no ghost in the cottage. No ghost at all. It had all been a bad dream.

But she knew that it hadn't *really* been a dream. She knew that she hadn't imagined it. There really *was* a ghost, and they had all seen it and spoken to it. The house really *was* haunted. By a ghost called Beryl.

Jessica looked nervously over her shoulder, half expecting to see the strange schoolgirl grinning behind her. But there was no one else in the room, apart from Martin and Lizzie. As she watched, Martin crossed to the board and took down the note that Jessica had left for the ghost. Lizzie was sitting at the table, looking as though she might burst into tears at any moment.

"Hey, Liz!" Jessica called. "Come and help Gareth with the drying up." Lizzie shot her a weak smile and stood up. Then she gave a little squeak of fright as the door suddenly swung open. Jessica shut her eyes quickly and muttered, "Oh, no, not again!" And then she heard her mother's voice and opened them.

"Haven't you finished that washing up yet?" her mother asked. "Hurry up, Jess. The sun's shining and it looks as though it's going to be a fine day at long last. We thought we'd make a picnic lunch and head for Sennen Cove and Land's End." She paused, and looked round at the others, a puzzled expression on her face. "Is anything wrong? You look — "

"*How* do we look?" Jessica asked quickly.

"Oh, I don't know," her mother said. "You all seem, well, sort of *stunned*. What's happened?"

"Nothing's happened," Martin said. "Nothing's happened at all. We're — we're just feeling a bit tired, that's all."

"Well then, some sea air will do you the world of good," Jessica's mother said briskly. "Come on, Martin. You can help me with the sandwiches."

Jessica turned back to the sink, and there was silence for a while as her mother and the others prepared the lunch. After a minute or two the door opened again and Andrew came in.

"Hurry up," he said. "We haven't got all day, you know."

"Oh, *do* keep quiet!" Jessica's mother said affectionately. "We're doing the best we can. Why don't you make yourself useful and fill the flask?"

Jessica heard him say, "Okay," and then, after a moment or two, "By the way, who's Beryl Bowditch?"

Gareth gasped, and dropped the cup he was drying. It smashed to pieces on the floor, shattering the shocked silence.

"Oh, *do* be careful, Gareth," his father said

wearily. "We have to pay Mrs Pengelly for any breakages, you know."

"Sorry," Gareth muttered, and bent down to pick up the pieces.

Martin said quickly, "What do you mean, Dad? How do you know about Beryl — " He stopped short then, silenced by a warning glance from Jessica.

Andrew looked puzzled. "There's a note on the board," he said. "Haven't you seen it?"

"No," Jessica said.

"It's a pretty stupid note," Andrew went on. "I'd have thought you kids were past that sort of thing."

"What sort of thing, Dad?" Martin said, trying to sound casual but not managing very well.

"Well, I ask you!" his father said. "Look at it. 'YOU ARE IN DEADLY DANGER. DON'T SAY I DIDN'T WARN YOU. SIGNED BERYL BOWDITCH (MISS).' That's pretty childish, if you ask *me*."

"It's just a joke," Jessica said, and then she gasped as someone dug her painfully in the ribs. She whirled round but there was no one near her.

And then a voice sounded in her ears, a familiar mocking voice that whispered, "So, I'm a joke, am I? Well, we'll soon see about *that*."

"Are you all right, Jess?" her mother asked.

"You've gone very pale. You're not sickening for something, are you?"

"N-no," Jessica stammered. "I'm all right. Really I am. Isn't it time we were going?" And she ran out of the room, away from the others and away from the mocking laughter in her ears that no one else could hear.

Jessica began to feel better once they had left the cottage and set off in the car. The others seemed to relax too, and the rest of the day passed pleasantly enough. They ate their lunch on the wide sweep of sand at Sennen Cove, and then went on to Land's End, which was shrouded in mist and cluttered with tourists. They didn't stay there long but drove on to Porthcurno, where they clambered happily over the steep stone tiers of the open-air theatre that was carved out of the cliffs overlooking the cove.

"They're not as bad as I thought," Lizzie said, as she and Jessica sat together on a granite seat, gazing down at the stage below, with its backdrop of grey seething sea.

"What aren't?" Jessica asked.

"The Monsters," Lizzie explained. "Martin and Gareth. They're quite nice when you get to know them, aren't they?"

Jessica didn't answer. She still hadn't forgiven Martin for finishing the Ricey-Pops.

It was only when they came in sight of the cottage once again that Jessica remembered the ghost and her heart sank. She dreaded the thought of going back inside, and of what they might find there. But, when at last she did go into the cottage, she was pleasantly surprised to discover that nothing seemed to have changed. She had fully expected to find the furniture overturned and all the windows broken but the house seemed to be undisturbed. It was only when she went into the kitchen and found her mother and Andrew laughing at a note on the board that she knew that Beryl hadn't been idle in their absence.

"All right," she said wearily. "What does it say this time?"

Her mother grinned at her. "Take a look for yourself," she said. "I didn't realize that you and Martin were *such* good friends, dear."

Jessica gave her a puzzled look and then turned to the board. On a large piece of paper, in bright red letters, was scrawled:

JESSICA LOVES MARTIN.
HA, HA, HA!

She stared at the note in horror, unable at first to believe her eyes, and then she ripped the note from the board and stalked out of the kitchen, her face burning with embarrassment. This time she knew that everyone could hear the laughter that followed her out of the room.

Jessica didn't dare look at Martin when they met again at supper time. Luckily he hadn't seen the note and she hoped that neither Andrew nor her mother would be tempted to tell him about it.

As she ladled spaghetti onto her plate, Jessica's mother smiled at her and whispered loudly, "It's all right, darling, your secret's safe with me."

Andrew said wickedly, "Ah, but is it safe with *me*?" and winked at her.

Jessica looked down at her plate, blushing furiously. She'd die if Andrew said anything about the note to Martin, she knew she'd just die.

But her luck was in. Andrew said nothing about it. Instead he started to talk about the places they might visit the next day if the weather stayed fine.

Andrew was busy singing the praises of a place called Bedruthan Steps when there was a sudden squawk from Gareth. Without any warning, his plate had tipped over, piling a steaming heap of spaghetti and meat sauce into his lap. Gareth shot to his feet, his eyes bright with pain and alarm. A thick mixture of spaghetti and sauce was dripping from his shirt and jeans.

"I — I — I didn't do it!" he gasped. "It wasn't me, I — "

"Oh, Gareth, how could you be so *clumsy*!" Jessica's mother stormed. "Look at the mess you're in! How on earth did you manage to upset your plate like that?"

"I didn't," he moaned miserably. "It wasn't me. Someone else pushed the plate. Someone pushed it . . ."

"Oh, don't be so stupid," his father said. "No one did anything of the sort. It was just pure clumsiness on your part. I don't know what's got into you, I really don't. Now go and get changed before you cause any more damage." Jessica stared down at her own plate as Gareth scurried from the room. She sneaked a glance at Martin under her lashes and saw him staring back at her, an anxious expression on his face.

"Well," Jessica's mother said. "I hope that's the last accident of the day."

But she was wrong. When Jessica got up to clear the plates from the table and carry them to the sink, she felt a hand grab her foot and she sprawled headlong across the kitchen floor. The dirty plates crashed around her in a shower of splintering crockery.

She lay on the floor for a moment, waiting to get her breath back, not daring to sit up and see her mother's face. When at last she got to her feet, her mother said faintly, "I don't believe it. I just *don't* believe it. What's got into all of you? What's going on?"

Jessica looked at her mother's angry, puzzled face and longed to tell her the truth. If only she could tell her mother that the house was haunted. If only she could tell her that a ghost had tipped Gareth's plate into his lap, that a ghost called Beryl, who wore a gym-slip and wire-rimmed spectacles, had tripped her up and had written those notes on the board. But she couldn't tell her mother anything. She couldn't tell her because she wouldn't believe it. And who could blame her? Jessica wouldn't have believed it herself.

Jessica didn't think for one moment that they'd heard the last of Beryl for that day. And she was right.

The screaming started in the middle of the night. Jessica leaped awake with a start, her heart hammering in her chest. She didn't know what time it was but it was pitch dark outside. She lay in bed for a moment, unable to believe that she really was hearing the shrill sharp screams that seemed to echo round the cottage. There were crashing noises too, and mysterious bumps and thuds, as if furniture was being dragged about.

Jessica switched on her bedside light and jumped out of bed. As she did so, Lizzie whispered, "What's happening, Jess? Who is it? Who's making all that noise?"

"I'll give you three guesses," Jessica muttered angrily, and opened the bedroom door. The noise seemed to be coming from the boys' room. As Jessica headed down the passage towards it, another door opened and Andrew came out.

"What's happening?" he asked. "What's going on?"

Jessica said nothing. Instead she pushed open the door of the room that Martin and Gareth shared. She gasped when she looked inside. It was a mess. Chairs had been overturned, clothes were scattered across the beds, and the wardrobe was lying on its side on the floor. Drawers had been emptied and their contents thrown around the room. The place looked as if it had been ransacked by vandals.

By now, Jessica's mother had joined them at the door. "Who was making all that . . ." she began, and then stopped when she saw the room.

"I might have known," she said angrily. "I might have known it would be them. I might have known that those boys would choose the middle of the night to play more of their stupid games."

"Where *are* they, anyway?" Andrew asked. The boys were nowhere to be seen. And then Martin's face appeared from under one of the beds. Gareth was there beside him. They both looked pale and frightened.

"I'll deal with you two in the morning!" Andrew thundered. "In the meantime, get this room tidied up before you do anything else." He turned and stalked out of the room. Jessica's mother gave the boys a puzzled frown before following Andrew back to their bedroom.

Jessica watched in silence as Martin and Gareth crawled from under the bed and started to tidy the room as best they could. "Was it — was it Beryl?" she asked at last.

"Yes," Martin said curtly. "Of course it was." He turned to look at her. "She wasn't joking, Jess. She really does mean business."

"Well, she's not getting the better of *me*," Jessica said defiantly. "I'm not going to be pushed around by — by someone who isn't *there*." And she bent down to help him lift the wardrobe from the floor.

* * *

43

Everyone was late for breakfast the next morning. For once, Jessica wasn't the last to arrive in the kitchen; as she sat down at the table she noticed that Gareth's chair was empty. No one said very much. Martin's face was pale and strained, and their parents both seemed very bad-tempered, as if they'd been quarrelling.

At last Andrew said, "I would have thought that after last night's little performance, you kids would have been satisfied. But it seems that you aren't. If you imagine that we're amused by your latest note then you'd better think again. We don't find it at all funny."

Jessica's heart sank. Oh no. Not another note. "What does it say?" she asked.

"Read it yourself," Andrew said, throwing a crumped piece of paper across the table towards her. "Although I expect you already know what it says. One or other of you must have written it."

Jessica stared at the note. It read:

I <u>DID</u> WARN YOU.
YOU'VE ONLY YOURSELVES TO BLAME.
GET OUT WHILE THE GOING IS GOOD.
B. BOWDITCH (MISS)

"I didn't write it," Jessica said. "I've never seen it before."

44

"Really?" Andrew said drily. "Well, it doesn't matter whether you did or not. What *does* matter is that this nonsense has got to stop. We're sick to death of your squabbles and these silly notes and all that noise and fighting in the night. You're ruining our holiday. In fact, we're seriously thinking of cutting it short and going back home early."

"*No!*" Jessica said quickly. "No, we mustn't go back. I want to stay here."

Her mother looked at her suspiciously. "You've changed your tune," she said. "Only the other day you said that you wanted to go back to London right away."

"I've changed my mind," Jessica said. "I — I like it here now. I really do." She didn't say that she wanted to go home more than anything else in the world, and that the only reason she wanted to stay was to prove that Beryl couldn't drive her away. She didn't say any of that. Instead she mumbled again, "I've changed my mind, that's all."

Her mother stared at her thoughtfully for a moment or two. "Well then," she said at last, "it's high time you children started to behave yourselves. If you don't, well, then we *will* go straight back home. And I'm not joking."

"What's happened to Gareth?" Andrew said then. "Give him a shout, Martin, will you?"

Martin nodded, and slipped out of the room. A moment later they heard him calling up the stairs to his brother. An answering shout told them that Gareth was on his way downstairs. And then they heard a sudden scream and the sound of someone falling. Andrew jumped to his feet just as Martin came rushing into the room, his face white with shock.

"Gareth's fallen down the stairs," he blurted out. "Oh, do come quick, Dad. He's hurt his leg, I think. He fell all the way down."

"Oh no!" Jessica's mother muttered as she followed Andrew into the hall. "That's all we need."

They found Gareth lying at the foot of the stairs, his face twisted with pain.

"My foot hurts," he moaned. "I can't get up."

"What happened?" Andrew asked. "You slipped, I suppose."

"No," Gareth said. "Someone pu — " Then he stopped short and said, "Yes, I slipped. I was — I was in a hurry and I slipped. I'm sorry, Dad."

"We'll get you to a doctor right away," Andrew said. "The sooner that foot's looked at the better. You've probably twisted it but we need to make sure that nothing's broken."

He carried Gareth straight out to the car, and Jessica's mother followed them. Before they drove away, she turned to Jessica and said, "I don't know how long we'll be. The rest of you had better finish your breakfast and then clear everything away. I'm sure you can find some way of occupying yourselves till we get back. Don't forget that Mrs Pengelly's just next door if you should need anything."

Jessica nodded, and she and Lizzie watched in silence as the car drove off. Then they went slowly back into the kitchen where they found Martin slumped at the table, gazing miserably into space.

When the girls came into the room, he looked up and said, "It's all getting beyond a joke now. Gareth didn't slip down the stairs. He told me that he was pushed. The ghost pushed him. And now he's badly hurt. He could have been killed. That girl could have killed him!"

"I know," Jessica said. "We've got to do something. We'd better call a truce."

"What do you mean, a truce?"

Jessica sat down beside him. "We've got to persuade her to stop the haunting. Before it's too late."

"She *won't* stop," Martin said. "She won't stop until we leave the cottage. She wants to get rid of us."

"I want to know why," Jessica said. "I want to find out why she hates us so much. And I want to tell her to stop the haunting."

"She won't listen," Lizzie said then. "She doesn't like us. She won't listen."

"We'll see about that." Jessica got up and crossed to the dresser. She found the notepad and a Biro and wrote:

WE WANT TO TALK TO YOU.
WE WANT TO CALL A TRUCE.
WE WANT TO BE YOUR FRIENDS.
PLEASE COME AND TALK TO US.

Then she pinned the page to the bulletin board and sat down again with the others.

"Let's see what happens now," she said. "It's worth a try, anyway. Let's see if the ghost comes back."

And they sat and waited in silence.

5

"She's not coming," Lizzie said. "I know she's not coming."

"Of course she is," Jessica said scornfully. "She'll be here any minute now. Just you wait and see."

Jessica hoped that she sounded more confident than she felt. They had been sitting round the kitchen table, waiting and listening, for at least ten minutes, and nothing had happened at all. It was rather like sitting in a dentist's waiting room, except that there weren't any old magazines to look at.

"She came right away, last time," Martin said doubtfully. "Are you sure this is going to work, Jess? Maybe Lizzie's right. Maybe the ghost won't come this time."

"Perhaps we've offended her," Lizzie suggested.

"Offended her?" Jessica was outraged. "Offended *her*? *She's* the one who's been causing all the trouble. *She's* the one who nearly killed Gareth. You really are a bonehead sometimes, Lizzie. *We're* the ones who should be offended, not her!" She raised her voice to a shout. "She's too scared to show herself, that's all it is! She's a coward! She hasn't got the guts to come out and talk to us!"

Martin cowered in his chair. "Do be careful, Jess. Don't overdo it."

"We don't want to make things worse," Lizzie said nervously. "We should try and be nice to her."

"You must be *joking*!" Jessica said angrily. "I'm not going to be nice to a coward. I'm not going to be at all nice to someone who pushes people down stairs. Someone," she added, remembering yesterday's message about her and Martin, "who writes disgusting notes about people and leaves them for anyone to see."

"What disgusting notes?" Martin asked eagerly. "I don't remember anything disgusting."

Jessica looked away quickly. "Oh, do shut up!" she said. "We ought to concentrate on getting the ghost to come back."

"We'll give her another five minutes," Martin said, looking at his watch. "If she's not here by then, we'd better — "

"Ssh!" Jessica said urgently. "Did you hear something?"

"What sort of something?" Martin asked, and then he gasped as the kitchen door whipped open and a gust of cold wind swept into the room. Then the door slammed shut with an ear-splitting bang, and Jessica jumped with fright.

"This is what happened last time," Martin murmured beside her, and she nodded, waiting for the shimmering figure to reappear, waiting for the strange girl in the old-fashioned school uniform to materialize in front of them. They stared nervously at the door but nothing happened. Nothing at all. No one appeared.

"Where is she?" Lizzie breathed at last. "I thought she was here. I thought — "

She was interrupted by a cackle of laughter that seemed to come from behind them. Jessica swung round in her chair and saw the girl. She was leaning nonchalantly against the cooker, gazing at them with a scornful expression on her thin face. She was wearing the same blue woollen stockings and creased and baggy black gym-slip, and her hair was as untidy as it had been before.

Her eyes glittered behind the wire-rimmed glasses as she said mockingly, "Well, that gave you something to think about, didn't it? I do like to keep people on their toes."

"You took your time," Martin said. "We've been waiting ages."

The girl scowled at him. "I'm not here at your beck and call, you know. Anyway, I wanted you to stew in your own juice for a bit." She paused, and then went on, "I don't know what you're complaining about, anyway. You're lucky I bothered to show myself at all. I didn't have to, you know."

"Why did you, then?" Jessica asked boldly.

The girl gave her a long stare. "I'm curious," she said at last. "I'm curious to know what you want."

There was a pause as Jessica and Martin each waited for the other to explain. In the end, it was Lizzie who said, "We want you to stop it."

Beryl looked at her contemptuously. "Oh you do, do you?"

"Yes. We want you to stop the haunting. It wasn't too bad when it was just notes on the board and making people drop cups and things but *we're* the ones who get into trouble when you start all that screaming at night. And now you've hurt Gareth. *Really* hurt him. And that's not fair."

Jessica stared at Lizzie in admiration then turned to Beryl. "Lizzie's right," she said. "Gareth might have been killed."

For the first time the ghost seemed a little unsure of herself. "Yes, well, perhaps that *was* going

52

a bit too far," she muttered, then she looked defiantly at Jessica and went on, "Well, there's one way you can stop it. You can go. You can leave this house."

Jessica glared at her. "I've already told you that we're *not* going," she said. "We're staying till the fortnight's up."

"Then you deserve all you get," Beryl snapped.

There was silence then as the children and the ghost scowled at each other. Then Beryl began to tap her foot impatiently. "Well, is that all?" she asked. "If you've nothing more to say then I'll — "

"No, stay!" Jessica said quickly. "*Please* stay." It was clear that the ghost wasn't going to take any notice of their complaints. They'd have to try some other way of persuading her to stop the haunting. "There's so much to talk about," she went on. "We'd like to get to know you better."

Beryl stopped tapping her foot. "Why do you want to get to know me?" she asked suspiciously.

"Because — because — " Jessica desperately tried to think of a convincing reason and failed. "Because we just do, that's all," she finished lamely.

Once again it was Lizzie who came to the rescue. "It's because you seem such an interesting person," she said. "I'm sure we could all learn such a lot from you. I'm sure you've got all sorts of interesting things to tell us."

Beryl looked down at her feet and gave a modest smile. "Yes, I expect I could," she said. "What do you want to know exactly?"

Lizzie opened and shut her mouth like a startled goldfish as she tried to think of something, and then Martin said, "Have — have you always been in this house? Is — was — is it your home?"

"I've always lived here," Beryl said, and then she started to walk towards them. The others stared at her open-mouthed as she drew out a chair and sat down at the table next to Martin. "You don't mind if I join you, do you?" she asked, smiling at him acidly.

"N-no," he said. "Of c-course not."

"There's no need to be scared," Beryl said. "I'm not going to bite you."

"No, but you *do* push people down stairs," Lizzie reminded her. "How would *you* like it if someone pushed *your* brother down stairs?" She thought for a moment and then added, "Have you — *did* you have a brother, by the way?"

"Yes," Beryl said. "I had a brother. And two sisters. I still have, as far as I know."

"They're still — alive?" Lizzie asked.

"Yes," said Beryl. "Henry, Vera and Ethel." Her face seemed to soften as she spoke of them and it seemed to Jessica that she began then to look more like an ordinary person and less like a ghost.

"What happened?" she asked gently.

"What d'you mean?" The dark eyes gleamed suspiciously at her.

"What happened — to *you*?" Jessica went on.

"I was riding home from school," Beryl said. "I was on my bicycle and a motor car came out of a side road without stopping. It crashed into my bike and sent me flying. I banged my head on the curb and, well, here I am — or rather, here I *aren't*!" She gave a little laugh and then coughed nervously. "I've been here ever since."

"Oh, you poor thing!" Lizzie said. "Your parents must have been awfully upset. And Henry and Vera and Ethel too."

"Yes, they were," Beryl said smugly. "They moved away to another house after a few weeks because they couldn't bear to live here without me. And I've been here on my own ever since."

"You must be very lonely," Jessica said.

Beryl shrugged. "I'm used to it."

"Perhaps," Jessica went on slyly, "you'd be less lonely if you were nicer to the people who come to stay here?"

"I don't *want* to be nice to them," Beryl said sullenly. "Why should I be? This is *my* house.

They've got no right to be here. *You've* got no right to be here." She laughed then, a harsh cackle that sent a shiver of fear down Jessica's spine. "Mind you, none of them stay very long. One or two notes on the board, a little midnight screaming, a few plates flying across the kitchen — it doesn't take much to send them on their way, believe me."

"Oh, I believe you," Martin said. "But you won't get rid of *us* so easily."

Beryl looked at him for a moment. "I'm beginning to think you may be right," she said seriously. "I can see that it's going to take more than a few screams to get rid of *you*." She shot him a sudden warm smile, and if it hadn't been for her old-fashioned clothes you would have thought that she was an ordinary person. "I'm sorry about your brother," she went on. "I hope he isn't badly hurt."

"So do I," Martin said.

"You're lucky," Beryl said then, and Jessica looked up in surprise at the note of sadness in her voice. "You're lucky having brothers and sisters. I wish mine were with me. I do miss them."

"How long have you — have you been here?" Jessica asked.

"The accident was in June 1925," Beryl said. "Work it out for yourself. I was never much good at arithmetic." She gave a sad little laugh. "It was three days after my birthday. I was twelve. I *am* twelve."

There was a pause and then, "Cripes!" Martin said. The others looked at him. He was staring at Beryl as though he couldn't believe his eyes. "You're — you're seventy-four years old, really," he said. "At least, that's how old you would have been if — "

"Yes, I thought it was something like that," Beryl said airily.

"You're the same age as my grandma," Lizzie said. "Isn't that nice? Mind you, you don't look a bit like her."

Beryl stared at her for a moment and then she threw back her head and let out a great roar of laughter. The others watched her for a moment and then, one by one, they joined in.

"I like you, Lizzie," Beryl said at last. "You remind me of my little sister, Ethel." She looked round at the others. "In fact I quite like all of you. Even Jessica. Perhaps I was wrong about you. I may even let you stay here. I'll think about it."

"Oh, *please* stop the haunting and let us stay," Lizzie said. "You're awfully nice when you're not pretending to be horrible."

Beryl laughed again. "I told you, I'll think about it."

"But how will we know when you've decided?" Lizzie asked.

"I'd have thought that was obvious," Beryl said. "When things stop happening, of course."

"But when — " Lizzie began, and then she stopped at the sudden sound of car doors slamming outside.

"That'll be Dad!" Martin said excitedly, running to the window. "Yes, it is. They're back and Gareth's with them. It looks as though he wasn't too badly hurt, after all." Jessica and Lizzie ran to join him at the window, and they watched in silence as Andrew helped Gareth from the back seat of the Volvo. His foot was bandaged but otherwise he seemed much the same as usual.

"Do come and look, Beryl," Lizzie said, turning round. "Gareth's come back and — oh, where is she?" The others turned. The room was empty. There was no sign of Beryl at all.

"She's gone." Lizzie's voice was heavy with disappointment. "I do wish she'd stayed. I was getting to like her."

"Don't worry, Liz," Jessica said, taking her hand. "She'll be back. I don't think we've seen the last of Beryl. I don't think we've seen the last of her at all."

6

A nd they hadn't. In the days that followed, Beryl kept popping up all over the place, or so it seemed, especially when they were least expecting her. Sometimes Jessica would only hear her voice, giggling wickedly in her ear or making rude remarks about one of the boys. At other times, always when the adults were out of the way, Beryl would appear without warning and join in whatever they were doing, almost as if she were one of the family. It was only when she grew bored that life became difficult in the cottage again. When that happened, Beryl would keep out of sight and it was then that rude notes would appear on the board once more, and everyone would be woken up in the middle of the night by unearthly shrieks and gibbering laughter. Luckily, no one was ever hurt again, although there was a nasty moment when she pulled Andrew's chair away just as he was about to sit down at the table and he fell and crashed his head on the stone tiles of the kitchen floor. But Gareth's accident seemed to have taught Beryl a lesson, and her hauntings now were rarely dangerous. In fact, they had all come to enjoy Beryl's unexpected visits. It was exciting to know that a ghost might suddenly appear to liven up a game of Scrabble or to start a pillow fight or just to sit companionably watching television.

Martin was the only one who seemed suspicious of Beryl's visits. "I never know what she's going to do next," he said to Jessica one day. "I think she's planning something. She used to be so awful and now — well, she's *different*."

"I know what you mean," Jessica said thoughtfully. "One minute she was telling us to get out of the cottage or else, and the next she's behaving as if she's our friend for life. Let's ask her what she's playing at next time she appears."

But Beryl only shuffled her feet and looked embarrassed when they asked her why things had changed. "I told you," she muttered. "I told you that I was going to think about whether you can stay or not."

"And you're still thinking?" Martin asked.

"Yes, I'm still thinking. I'll let you know when I've decided."

"But we want to know *now*," Martin persisted.

"Then you'll just have to be patient," Beryl snapped, and her dark eyes glittered dangerously. "And if you don't like it, you can just — "

Lizzie came in then to tell her that she was going to miss the beginning of *Neighbours* if she wasn't careful, and a nasty moment was averted. Beryl loved television. In her opinion, it was the best thing to have happened in the world since 1925.

Jessica watched her run from the room and then turned to Martin. "Do be careful," she said. "We don't want to spoil everything."

Martin scowled. "I just want to know, that's all. I just want to know if she's a friend or an enemy."

"At the moment she's a friend," Jessica said. "Let's just leave it at that."

The children weren't the only ones to appreciate the relaxed atmosphere in the cottage. Their parents, too, were more friendly and less irritable now that the hauntings had stopped.

"I can't believe it," Jessica's mother kept saying. "I can't believe that you children seem to be getting on so well now. I hope you're not plotting something. I hope there isn't going to be any more of that screaming in the middle of the night."

"Oh, don't be so silly, Mum," Lizzie said loftily then. "We've grown out of that sort of thing now."

"I do hope so. This is turning out to be a really good holiday. Especially now that the weather's improved so much."

The constant rain that had spoiled their first days at the cottage had now been replaced by brilliant warm sunshine, and they all spent as much time as they could on the beach.

"I know it's probably only a coincidence," Jessica said to Martin as they clambered over the rocks at the cove one morning, "but have you noticed that the weather got better as soon as Beryl stopped being so nasty? You don't think there's any connection, do you?"

Martin considered. "I shouldn't think so," he said at last. "It's just one of those things, I expect."

But Jessica wasn't altogether convinced. She wouldn't put anything past Beryl, not even influencing the weather. She decided to ask her about it when the ghost joined them in the kitchen after tea that evening, then she changed her mind. It was a stupid idea. A ghost couldn't possibly control the rain or sunshine. Or could she? Then she forgot about the weather altogether as she listened to Lizzie telling Beryl about their plans for the next day.

"We're going off in the car," she was saying happily, "and we're taking a picnic lunch and our swimming things. Andrew wants to see some old castle somewhere but we're going to spend most of the time on the beach. What a pity you can't come with us, Beryl."

Beryl smiled. "Perhaps I could," she said thoughtfully.

There was a sudden silence. Jessica had a vision of Beryl prancing about on a beach, dressed in an old-fashioned bathing costume, and let out a yelp of laughter.

Beryl scowled at her and said again, "Perhaps I *could* come with you."

"I — I didn't know — er — you could travel about," Martin said. "I thought ghosts only stayed in one place."

"The place they're haunting," Gareth added helpfully.

"Well, we *do* stay put, on the whole," Beryl said, "but we *are* able to move about if we want. It's not easy, though. We can do it if something from the haunt is moved. Then we can travel with it."

"I don't understand," Lizzie said plaintively.

"Don't be stupid *all* your life, Lizzie," Jessica said. "It's simple. If we want to take Beryl to the beach we can only do it if we take with us something that belongs to the house. Then she can — er — travel with it."

"You mean we'd have to take a chair or a wardrobe or something like that?"

"I suppose so," Jessica said.

She looked questioningly at Beryl who said, "It doesn't have to be as big as that. It could be something smaller, like a cushion or an ornament. Just as long as it belongs to the house."

"The little black china cat in the sitting room," Lizzie said. "Would that do? It's one of the nicest things in the cottage."

Beryl nodded. "Oh, yes. Anything like that will be fine. As long as it comes from the house. That's the important thing."

Lizzie looked round at the others, her eyes shining with delight. "That's settled then," she said. "Beryl's coming with us tomorrow. Isn't it exciting!"

When they set off the next morning, it seemed hard to believe that Beryl was actually travelling with them in the Volvo. They couldn't see her, of course, and she took care not to make any sound at all because Jessica's mother and Andrew were so close. But they knew she was there. Lizzie had tucked the small black china cat into the bottom of the bag that held the swimming things and books, and it was strange to think that a ghost was able to travel about with them just because

64

they had brought along that ordinary little ornament.

They carried the little black cat with them everywhere that day, and with it went Beryl. They carried the cat to the picturesque village of Port Isaac and then to the ruins of Tintagel Castle and then on to Bossiney, where they had a swim and then ate their lunch on the beach. After that, the children stayed on the sand while the grownups went to look for a waterfall among the trees in nearby Rocky Valley.

Beryl kept out of sight until Andrew and Jessica's mother had gone, and only then did she consent to appear and join the others on the sand. It was strange to see her there, away from the cottage, and she seemed ill at ease at first. But it didn't take long for her nervousness to disappear and she was soon running about on the beach with Lizzie, and helping her search for sea creatures in the rock pools.

It was when they were on their way home, slumped sleepily in the Volvo, that Jessica's mother turned round and said, "I see you picked up a friend on your travels today, Jessica. Odd-looking child, I thought. Who was she?"

"What — er — who? I mean, I don't know," Jessica said wildly, and Lizzie piped up at the same time, "What child? There wasn't any child with us," and Martin added, "We were by ourselves all the time."

"Don't all talk at once!" Jessica's mother laughed, covering her ears with her hands. Then, when an uneasy silence had fallen, she went on, "But I *saw* a girl with you. When Andrew and I got back from our walk there was a girl with you on the beach. Funny-looking creature. I could have sworn that she was wearing a gym-slip but I must have been imagining it. After all, no one wears gym-slips these days and certainly not on a *beach*. Did you see her, Andrew?"

"Can't say I did," Andrew muttered.

"Well, *I* saw her all right. A glimpse of her, anyway. She seemed to disappear after that. Who was she, Jess?"

"Dunno," Jessica mumbled. "Just some girl or other. One minute she was there, sort of. And the next she wasn't. I didn't ask what her name was."

"Oh, I see," her mother said. "Odd-looking child, I thought." Then she started to talk to Andrew about something else.

Jessica breathed a sigh of relief and sank back on the seat with her eyes closed.

Then, suddenly, a voice in her ear said, "Odd-looking child, indeed!" and Jessica quickly opened her eyes again.

"I don't look at all odd," Beryl went on. *"She's*

a fine one to talk. Any woman with hair *that* colour is in no position to call anyone else *odd*."

"All right, all right," Jessica whispered furiously. "Now just keep quiet or you'll ruin everything."

Her mother turned round again. "Did you say something, dear?"

"No," Jessica said. "I was just talking to — to myself, that's all."

"Oh, that's all right then."

And the car purred on towards the cottage.

It was while they were getting ready for bed that night that Lizzie first mentioned the party. She had been chattering for ages about nothing in particular and Jessica hadn't really been listening. But when Lizzie said, "So I think it would be *really* nice if we gave her a party," Jessica sat up with a start and said, "Party? What party? What on earth are you talking about, Liz?"

Lizzie sighed heavily. "Haven't you been listening to a word I've been saying? I said it would be nice if we could find Henry and Vera and Ethel."

"Who on earth are — oh yes, Beryl's brother and sisters. But why should we try and find them?"

"Because Beryl misses them so," Lizzie said

patiently. "You know how lonely she is and how she envies us having a sister and brothers."

"*Step*brothers," Jessica reminded her.

"Yes, all right, *step*brothers then. Anyway, they're family, whatever they're called. I thought it would be a good idea if we looked for them and invited them here so that Beryl could see them. We could give a party."

Jessica thought about it. It was a mad idea but it *would* be interesting to see what Beryl's family were like . . .

"But how would we go about finding them? We don't know where they live."

"We'll find a way," Lizzie said. "Anyway, it'd be worth trying, wouldn't it?"

"And what do we say to them when — *if* we find them? Good afternoon, you don't know who we are but would you like to come to a party at our house and meet your dead sister who's a ghost? Oh, don't be stupid, Liz. Look, it's getting late and I'm ti — "

"We wouldn't say *that*!" Lizzie said indignantly. "Of course they wouldn't come if we told them about the ghost. No, we'd tell them — we'd tell them something else."

"What?"

"I don't know," Lizzie said sleepily. "We'll think of something. Anyway, *I* think it's a lovely idea.

Let's see what the Monsters think about it to-morrow."

"Yes," Jessica said. "We'll see what they think tomorrow." She smiled to herself as she pictured Martin's reaction to Lizzie's latest harebrained scheme. He'd laugh himself silly . . .

"I think it's a great idea," Martin said. "Clever of you to think of it, Lizzie."

Jessica stared at him open-mouthed. She couldn't believe her ears.

"It'll be really interesting to try and find the brother and sisters," Martin went on enthusiastically. "Even if we don't have a party, it'll be fun trying to track them down."

"Oh, we *must* have a party." Lizzie sounded disappointed. "It won't be worth doing if they don't come to the house so that Beryl can see them."

"We could take *her* to *them*," Gareth suggested. "She could travel with the cat like she did yesterday."

"No, it'll be easier if they come here," Martin said. "Then they can have a grand family reunion, all four of them."

"Oh, *very* touching, I must say!" Jessica sneered. "And what makes you think they're going to come here, even if we *do* manage to find

69

them? What makes you think they're going to come to a strange house just because *you* ask them?"

"But it isn't a strange house," Gareth pointed out. "They lived here once, remember? This used to be their home."

"That's it!" Martin said excitedly. "We'll tell them that we thought they might like to come and have a cup of tea in the family home. For old times' sake. They probably haven't been here for years. I bet they're dying to see how much it's changed."

"I still think it's a stupid idea," Jessica said gloomily but no one else seemed to agree with her. The others all decided that the plan should go ahead. Of course, there was always a chance that they wouldn't be able to find Henry and his sisters or, if they did, that none of the old people would accept the invitation. They'd have to wait and see.

"Now then," Martin said, sitting down at the kitchen table, "how are we going to find Henry and the others?"

"Ask at the post office," Gareth suggested. "Or at that little supermarket in the village."

"I know," said Lizzie. "Let's ask Mrs Pengelly first. She's lived here all her life, or so she said. She's bound to know everyone in the village."

"You really are a genius, Liz," Martin said admiringly. "We'll go and ask her as soon as we've cleared these breakfast things away. Now then, whose turn is it to do the washing up?"

"Yours," said Jessica.

They found Mrs Pengelly in her garden, gazing despondently at the lawn, which was in urgent need of mowing. She lived right next door to the cottage in a neat modern bungalow which had been built on ground that was once part of the cottage garden.

"We used to live here ourselves," she'd told them when they arrived at the cottage at the beginning of the holiday. "But we — we decided we wanted something more convenient and so we built the bungalow instead."

Jessica, remembering that conversation now, wondered whether Beryl had driven Mrs Pengelly away from the cottage. Then she turned to listen to Martin, who was talking to the old lady about the weather.

"Enjoying your holiday, are you?" Mrs Pengelly asked after a while, and then, when they all assured her that they were loving every minute of it, she went on cautiously, "I hope you're finding the cottage comfortable."

"Oh, yes," Lizzie said. "It's so peaceful here, isn't it?"

Mrs Pengelly nodded and said, "You haven't — you haven't heard anything *odd*, have you?"

"What do you mean?" Jessica asked, knowing perfectly well what she meant.

"Oh, noises in the night. That sort of thing."

"Oh, *no!*" they all replied in chorus, and Mrs Pengelly smiled with relief.

"Good," she said. "I did wonder. Other people who've stayed there have — no, take no notice. I just wondered, that's all."

"Wondered what?" Jessica asked innocently.

"Oh, nothing. It's just that some people who've rented the cottage in the past have — they've left early, that's all. They haven't stayed for the full time they've booked.

"I can't think why," Martin said. "It's a lovely cottage, so comfortable and very historic, I should think. Have you owned it a long time?"

"Oh, about six years," Mrs Pengelly said. "Before that it belonged to my husband's family."

"Did they build it?" Martin asked.

"Goodness me, no. They bought it years ago, oh, way back in the 1920s, I think. A local family lived here then." She frowned at Martin and said, "Why do you want to know? Why are you so interested in the cottage?"

There was a pause. Jessica squirmed with embarrassment, hoping that Martin would come up with a convincing explanation. He did.

"It's — it's for a project at school," he said at last. "We have to investigate the history of a house. Any house. We have to find out as much about it as we can — all the people who've lived there over the years, the way the house has changed, that sort of thing." He shot Mrs Pengelly an angelic smile. "Your cottage is so interesting that I thought it would be ideal for the project. That's why I want to find out about the people who've lived there."

Mrs Pengelly seemed impressed. "Well, *I* don't know very much about it," she said slowly. "I might have some old photos . . ."

"What about the family who owned it before you?" Martin said carefully. "Perhaps *they* could help. If they still live in the village, that is."

"Oh yes, they're still here," Mrs Pengelly said. "Well, the parents are dead, of course. But old Henry Bowditch lived here as a child. He's still in the village. And so is a sister of his. She runs that funny old junk shop by the post office. What's it called? This and That? Bits and Pieces? Something like that, anyway. Vera Thrush she's called now but she used to be Vera Bowditch. You could try asking them."

"Odds and Ends," Lizzie said.

"What, dear?"

"Odds and Ends. That shop in the village is called Odds and Ends."

"Of *course* it is." Mrs Pengelly beamed at her. "Anyway, you go and have a word with Vera. And Henry too, of course. I'll give you his address. They'll be able to tell you all about the cottage." She paused and smiled at them. "I must say it makes a pleasant change to find young people taking an interest in the community instead of leaving litter around and playing that nasty pop music. Now I really must get on with this lawn. Let me know how you get on, won't you?"

As they walked down the neat path to the front gate, Martin turned to Jessica and grinned at her in triumph. "Well, that was easy, wasn't it?" he said. "So far, so good."

"That was the easy part," she said loftily. "It's persuading the old people to come to the cottage that'll be the problem."

"It'll be a piece of cake," Martin said confidently. "Just you wait and see."

7

"You've *what?*" Jessica's mother said. "You've done *what?*"

Jessica gulped, and repeated, "We've invited some old people here for tea tomorrow."

Her mother sat down and said weakly, "I don't believe it. I just don't believe it."

"It — it's true," Jessica mumbled. She looked down at the floor, wishing that it would open up and swallow her for ever.

Her mother closed her eyes and said, "It's not true. It's all a dream. When I open my eyes it'll be this morning again and none of this will have happened . . ." She opened her eyes again. "Tell me it's not true, Jessica. Tell me I'm dreaming."

"It isn't a dream," Jessica said. "They're coming to tea tomorrow. Three of them."

"But why, Jess? *Why?*"

Jessica stared at her mother, wondering how best to explain the situation. Martin had been right — persuading the old people to come to the house had been a piece of cake compared with telling their parents about it. They hadn't considered this particular difficulty when they were making their plans for Beryl's tea party.

"It's — it's for Martin's school project," Jessica said at last, hoping that her mother would swallow this explanation as easily as Mrs Pengelly had done.

"Martin's school project? What's that got to do with old people *here*, for heaven's sake?"

"Nothing. I mean, quite a lot."

Her mother began to sound impatient. "Make up your mind, Jessica," she said.

"It's the house, really," Jessica went on quickly. "He's got to do a project on the history of a house and so he chose this one."

"Why *this* house? Why didn't he choose someone else's? What about his *own*?"

Jessica gaped at her desperately and then went on: "*I* don't know. He says this one's more interesting. Anyway, we're helping him to find out about the history of the cottage and all that sort of thing. And so we found these three old people who used to live here and we've invited them here for tea tomorrow so that we can talk to them about what the house was like when they were children.

And *that's* why they're coming," she finished defiantly.

Her mother stared at her open-mouthed. She started to say something and then changed her mind. Then she stood up and crossed to the window. She stared out at the garden for a moment or two and then turned. She was smiling.

"Well, I can't deny I'm surprised, Jessica. It all seems *very* odd. But if that's what you want to do, then I can't see any reason why these people shouldn't come to tea. I do wish you'd asked our permission *first*, though, instead of telling me afterwards."

Jessica stared at the floor again and mumbled, "Sorry."

"You'll have to organize everything yourself, of course."

Jessica looked up in surprise. "What do you mean?"

"The tea party was your idea and so it's up to you to make the tea and decide what you're going to eat and all that sort of thing. This party is your idea, not ours, so it's only fair that you should organize it. Andrew and I will go out for the afternoon and leave you all to it."

"But — " Jessica began, but her mother went on firmly, "No buts about it, Jessica. We'll give you some money towards the food but that's as far as it'll go. The rest is up to you and the others."

Jessica smiled at her weakly and said, "Thanks, Mum. I knew you'd understand."

Her mother gave her a long serious look and then said, "Did you, indeed?" Then she added, "Tell me one thing, though. How on earth did you persuade the old people to come? They must have thought you were out of your minds!"

"Oh, it wasn't as bad as that," Jessica said. "They seemed very pleased to be asked."

This wasn't quite true. Mrs Thrush had indeed seemed pleased once she had stopped being puzzled but, from what Martin had said, Henry Bowditch's reaction had been much more suspicious.

It had been decided the day before that Jessica and Lizzie would go and speak to Vera Thrush at her shop while Martin went to find Henry Bowditch at the address Mrs Pengelly had given them. They hoped that Vera or Henry would then be able to tell them how to find Ethel. Gareth had to stay at the cottage because his injured ankle made walking difficult and the doctor had told him to rest it as much as possible.

Vera Thrush had turned out to be a large old lady with bright red hair and far too much make-up. It took the girls some time to pluck up enough courage to speak to her so they spent a good twenty minutes investigating the contents of her untidy shop before Jessica at last explained the real reason for their visit.

The old lady had stared at her blankly for a moment or two at first, and then she smiled and said, "Well, that's very kind of you, I must say. Are you sure your parents won't mind? It'll be nice to see inside the cottage again, I don't mind telling you. I've often wondered how much it's changed. I haven't been inside that house for, oh, I don't know, it must be going on for sixty years now. We had happy times there as kids."

"So you'll come to tea, then?" Lizzie had said.

"Bless you, dear, of course I will. And I'll persuade that old grouch Henry to come as well. I'm sure Ethel will be pleased too."

"We haven't spoken to her yet," Jessica said. "We don't know where to find her."

"Oh, she lives in that row of houses just past the garage. Mrs Hazelbury she is now, of course. But I'll be seeing her this dinner time, anyway, so I'll speak to her, if you like. What time do you want us to come?"

"About four o'clock," Lizzie said.

"I'll have to shut the shop early but that won't matter. I couldn't miss a chance to see inside the cottage after all these years." She gave them a broad grin, revealing two rows of yellow teeth, several of which were missing. Then she said, "Are you *quite* sure your parents don't mind? Perhaps I'd better speak to them first — "

"No, they don't mind at all," Jessica said quickly, and Lizzie added, "They think it's a wonderful idea."

"Well, that's all right then," Mrs Thrush said. "We'll see you for tea the day after tomorrow."

It had all been as simple as that. When Jessica and Lizzie compared notes with Martin later on, however, they learned that he hadn't been so lucky. Henry Bowditch had turned out to be a fierce old gentleman who lived all by himself in a very small cottage that smelled of stale fish and cigarette smoke. He wouldn't listen to Martin at first, and he threatened to call the police if he didn't clear off. But Martin had persisted, and the old man had finally agreed to come to tea, on condition that his two sisters would be there too.

"So they'd better turn up," Martin said to Jessica. "There'll be hell to pay otherwise. Henry's a tough old stick, believe me."

"Vera's nice, though," Lizzie said. "Except for all that lipstick. She doesn't look a bit like Beryl, does she?"

"Well, how can she?" Jessica said scornfully. "Beryl's twelve and Vera's — well, she must be nearly eighty. How can they possibly look the same?"

Jessica remembered that conversation now as she assured her mother once again that the old people had eagerly accepted the invitation to tea. And it reminded her that there was still one more person to be consulted.

"Well, thanks, Mum," she said. "I'll just go and find the others and tell them the good news."

Martin, Gareth and Lizzie were waiting anxiously for her in the garden.

"It's okay!" Jessica said breathlessly when she joined them. "She doesn't mind. *We* have to do the tea, though. She and Andrew will be going out for the afternoon."

"Good thing too," Gareth said. "We'd have been sunk if they'd decided to join in."

"So all we have to do now is buy cakes and things," Lizzie said. "Let's have chocolate éclairs. I *love* chocolate éclairs."

"I'll make a trifle," Martin said. "I make terrific trifles. What else shall we have?"

"Ice cream," said Jessica. "And we can open some tins of peaches and things."

"We could buy one of those squidgy cream cakes from the baker's in the village," Gareth said.

"*Two* cream cakes!" Martin shouted.

"*Three!*" Jessica screeched excitedly. Then she fell silent as she remembered the person who still hadn't been told about their plans.

"What's the matter?" Martin asked.

"We haven't told Beryl," Jessica said. "We've got to invite Beryl. If she isn't there then it'll all be a waste of time."

"Let's put a note on the board," Gareth suggested.

They ran inside the cottage and Jessica found the notepad and pen and sat down to word the invitation. Then they pinned it up on the bulletin board and stood back to admire it:

YOU ARE INVITED TO A SURPRISE
TEA PARTY.
TOMORROW AFTERNOON
AT FOUR O'CLOCK
R.S.V.P.

"What does R.S.V.P. mean?" Lizzie asked.

"It means that she has to reply," Martin said. "She has to tell us whether she'll be coming to the party or not."

"What do we do if she doesn't want to come?" Jessica asked.

"We'll have to go ahead just the same," Martin said. "Otherwise the parents will get suspicious."

"But how is Beryl going to R.S.V.P.?" Lizzie asked. "How's she going to tell us?"

"Oh, don't worry about that," Jessica said loftily. "Beryl will find a way."

And she did. When Jessica looked at the board that evening before supper, she found that the invitation had disappeared. In its place hung another note that read:

I'LL BE THERE.
JUST MAKE SURE
THERE ARE PLENTY
OF JAM DOUGHNUTS.

8

"Well, I think it all looks terrific!" Martin said, admiring the laden table in the sitting room. "I think we've remembered everything. Cakes, biscuits, ice cream, peaches, éclairs, jam tarts, and last but not least a magnificent trifle made by yours truly."

"Where are the doughnuts?" Jessica asked. "Beryl specially asked for jam doughnuts."

"Don't worry," Martin said. "They're over there, next to the macaroons. Now then, what about the cups and saucers and things?"

"Oh, I'm leaving those in the kitchen. It'll be easier to pour out the tea there and bring the cups in. What's the time?"

"Five to four. They'll be here any minute now."

Jessica went to the window and peered out. "I do hope it's all going to work. Do you think we're doing the right thing?"

"Of course we are," Martin said. "I just hope

Beryl appreciates it. This *is* all for her benefit, after all."

"I wonder if she'll turn up," Jessica said. As if in answer to her question, the door whipped open and a chilly gust of wind surged into the room, blowing a pile of paper napkins from the table on to the carpet. Jessica bent down to pick them up and then, when she stood up again, she saw that Beryl was leaning against the doorpost, looking at them suspiciously.

"Well, I'm here," she said. "When does this so-called party begin?"

"When the others arrive," Jessica said briskly. She gave Beryl a critical glance. She was still wearing the same creased black gym-slip. You'd think she'd have worn something else in honour of the occasion but perhaps ghosts didn't change their clothes. She must remember to ask her one day when they had more time to talk.

"Others? What others?" Beryl snapped. "You didn't say that anyone else was coming."

"Oh, didn't I?" Jessica said innocently. "How silly of me. We've invited a couple of other people, that's all. I'm sure you'll enjoy meeting them."

"I'm not meeting anyone!" Beryl said, and immediately began to shimmer and fade, a sure sign that she was about to disappear.

"Don't go!" Martin shouted, but the ghost took

no notice. Soon only a slight ripple in the air showed that she had been in the room at all.

"Oh no!" Jessica groaned. "What are we going to do? It'll be *hopeless* if she isn't here. What are — "

"Don't worry," Beryl's voice said then. "I'm still here all right. I'm not going to show myself, that's all. I want to find out what you're up to. I want to know what this so-called tea party is all about." There was a pause, and when she spoke again her voice had grown more sinister. "I hope you're not trying any funny business. I hope you're not going to do anything stupid. I really do hope so."

"We're not!" Martin said. "We're giving this tea party for *you*. We've gone to a lot of trouble, all for your benefit, and the very least you can do — "

"They're here!" Lizzie said excitedly, popping her head round the door. "They're coming up the path now."

Jessica felt a sharp pang of guilt when she opened the front door and saw Henry Bowditch and his sisters standing in the porch. They had obviously gone to a lot of trouble to look smart for the occasion: the old man was wearing a shiny white collar and a dark blue suit that seemed to be a couple of sizes too big for him, and the face of the little grey-haired woman beside him was completely shadowed by an elaborate hat covered in cherries and artificial ferns. She was presumably Ethel Hazelbury, Beryl's younger sister. Vera Thrush had put on another layer of make-up and was wearing a patterned purple dress that made her look like a sofa on legs.

"Good — good afternoon," Jessica said. "We're so glad you could come. Won't you come in? Martin, take Mrs Hazelbury's coat, will you?"

Jessica stood aside to let the old people past into the hall and, as she did so, she was suddenly aware of a noise in her ear that sounded like a sharp intake of breath. She waited until the others had disappeared into the sitting room before saying, "Beryl?" very hesitantly. But there was no answer and so she shrugged and followed the old people inside.

"Well, it doesn't seem to have changed much," Henry Bowditch said, looking round the sitting room.

"It seems smaller, somehow," Ethel said. "The furniture's different, of course. And the wallpaper. But I can remember it as if it was yesterday."

"Can we see the rest of the cottage?" Mrs Thrush asked.

"Oh, yes, of course," Jessica said, and led the way out of the room on the first stage of what was to be a long conducted tour of the house and garden. By the time they all arrived back in the sitting room, the old people were talking nineteen to the dozen. The party may have been intended for Beryl's benefit but her brother and sisters were certainly enjoying themselves.

"Well, that was *marvellous*!" Vera said, sinking into an armchair. "It really brings it all back, seeing the old place again." She caught sight then of the table laden with food. "And look at that spread! Don't tell me it's all for us?"

"Yes, of course it is," Jessica said. "Do help yourselves, please. I'll just go and put the kettle on. I'm sure you'd all like some tea."

"I thought you'd never ask," Mr Bowditch growled, and then grinned at her.

"I'll come and help you," Lizzie said, and followed her into the kitchen.

"Well, *they* all seem to be having a whale of a time," Jessica said as she filled the kettle. "I wish I could be sure that Beryl was. She's keeping very quiet."

"I hope she's still here," Lizzie said.

"I'm here all right," snapped a familiar voice, and the girls turned to see Beryl standing in the doorway, her arms akimbo and her eyes glittering behind her round glasses. "I'd like to know what's going on," she said. "Who *are* those dreadful old people?"

Jessica gaped at her. "Don't you recognize them?"

"Recognize them? Why should I recognize them? I've never seen them before in my life."

Lizzie laughed. "Of course you have. They're Henry and Ethel and Vera."

Beryl stared at her blankly.

"Your brother and sisters," Lizzie said. "Surely you recognize them."

It was the first time either of the girls had seen Beryl at a loss for words. Her mouth dropped open and she looked suddenly afraid and lost. But then, almost at once, her thin mouth snapped shut again and a metallic gleam returned to her eyes.

"Don't talk nonsense. Those old fools aren't my brother and sisters," she said.

"But they are," Jessica persisted. "Henry and Ethel and Vera. Ethel's married now, of course, and Vera was too but — "

"You're lying!" Beryl screeched. "They're *not* my family! They're not!"

"But they *are*," Lizzie insisted.

"How can they be? Ethel was a sweet little girl with fair curls and big blue eyes. She wasn't anything like that silly old hag in the awful hat. And as for the other one, that fat cow in the purple with all that paint slapped on her face, you're not trying to tell me — "

"That's Vera," Jessica said. "She *is* Vera."

"*They are not my family!*" Beryl's eyes were blazing with hate and Jessica felt suddenly uneasy. She'd known it wouldn't work. She'd known that the party would be a disaster. It was all going wrong . . .

"Listen, Beryl, don't you understand?" Lizzie said quietly. "You only remember Henry and the others as they were when you last saw them. They were children then. But that was over sixty years ago and they've grown old since then. They aren't children any more."

"I don't believe you," Beryl said, but she didn't sound as certain now.

"We wanted you to meet them," Lizzie went on. "We thought you'd like to see your own brother and sisters again. Stay with us for a bit longer. You'll see that they really *are* your family. We'll prove it to you."

"But they *aren't!*" Beryl said. "They *can't* be. Those ugly old people are nothing to do with me. Nothing!"

"Promise me you'll wait and see," Lizzie begged. "Promise you'll listen to what they say and . . ." She stopped then, as Beryl faded swiftly out of sight, and then she turned to Jessica. "I did my best," she said.

"Of course you did, Liz. I'm sure she'll stay.

Now then, we'd better pour out this tea before they start screaming for it."

By the time Jessica and Lizzie were able to sit down again with the others, conversation was beginning to flag. None of the old people seemed to have eaten very much and only Vera Thrush appeared to be enjoying herself now.

"Well, that was a lovely cup of tea," she said, putting down her cup. "But I really think we should be going now. It's been ever so interesting seeing the house but — "

"*No!*" Martin said quickly. "You must have another cup of tea. And how about a doughnut? Or some of that jam sponge. And you haven't touched the trifle. I made it myself. Specially."

"I really couldn't eat another thing," Mrs Thrush said. "But I wouldn't mind another cup of tea, if you really insist."

Jessica took the old lady's cup and went into the kitchen to refill it. When she came back, she said loudly, "Tell us about your family. Did you have any other brothers and sisters?"

Mrs Hazelbury looked at her in surprise. "We had another sister," she said hesitantly, "but she died very young."

"Beryl her name was," Henry Bowditch said.

"How — how did she die?" Jessica asked. "I mean, was it an illness or something — "

"It was an accident," Vera Thrush put in. "She was knocked off her bicycle on her way home from school."

"Oh, how *awful*!" Lizzie said loudly, hoping that Beryl was taking all this in. "The poor little girl! What a dreadful thing to happen!"

"It was her own fault," Henry said grumpily. "Wasn't watching where she was going, silly little cow. Deserved all she got."

There was a sudden shocked silence and then Ethel said quickly, "It seems unkind, I know, and one shouldn't really speak ill of the dead but," and here she lowered her voice to a whisper, "none of us really liked Beryl. Nasty little girl she was. I don't think anyone missed her at all."

There was a pause and then Jessica said desperately, "But — but she was only a child. She couldn't have been as awful as you say, surely?"

"Oh, she *was*, dear," Vera said. "None of us liked her. Proper little madam, she was. Too clever for her own good *and* cheeky with it. And there was a nasty streak to her nature too. I always remember — " She stopped short and let out a loud screech as her cup suddenly fell from her hand, emptying its contents into her large purple lap.

Jessica leaped to her feet. "Don't worry!" she

said. "I'll get a cloth." She headed for the door and then turned at the sound of a loud crash. A picture had fallen from the wall and now lay on the carpet. And then, as she watched in horror, the lights suddenly began to switch themselves on and off without stopping.

"What — what's going on?" Henry Bowditch growled, jumping to his feet.

"It's an earth tremor," Ethel Hazelbury said. "It must be."

Her brother glared at her. "In Cornwall? Don't be so stupid."

Jessica turned back to the door but found that she couldn't open it. There was another crash behind her, and another, and another. One by one the plates on the table lifted into the air and then smashed into smithereens against the wall. Cakes and tarts and biscuits flew through the air, and Jessica blinked in amazement as a large cream cake landed right in the centre of Vera Thrush's face. The old lady squawked and gasped for breath, and then Henry gave a shout as a jam doughnut caught him on the side of the head, followed swiftly by another. Jessica ducked as a doughnut flew in her direction and then she crawled into a corner by the window where Lizzie was already cowering.

"I told you this was a rotten idea," Jessica muttered. "I've got a funny feeling that Beryl isn't enjoying this party very much."

"And we know now why she wanted us to buy jam doughnuts," Lizzie said thoughtfully, and then she screamed as Martin's bowl of trifle hovered over her head. It turned upside down, and a sticky slimy mess slithered over her hair and face.

By now Henry was tugging feebly at the door handle, with Ethel and Vera close behind, moaning in terror as doughnuts and macaroons and chocolate éclairs shot through the air around them. And then the lights stopped flashing and the room began to darken. As it did so, a hideous moaning filled the air, an unearthly sound that droned on and on until it ended in a terrifying high-pitched shriek. Jessica caught sight of a face in the darkness, a huge hideous scaly face with staring hollow eyes and a gaping smile before she covered her eyes and shrank back in her corner, not daring to look up, hoping desperately that the thing she had seen wouldn't come near her.

Slowly, slowly, the shrieking stopped and the room lightened. For a moment or two, Jessica kept her eyes closed. Then, when all she could hear was a low sobbing, she looked up at last. Henry, Vera and Ethel were crouched in terror near the door. Around them, the room was a mess of overturned furniture and broken crockery, with the remains of cakes and jelly splattered on the ceiling, walls, chairs and the carpet.

And then, as Jessica watched, the air shimmered and shook and Beryl appeared as if from nowhere, glowering at her brother and sisters as they crouched against the wall. Vera looked up, and her eyes widened in astonishment when she saw her. Beryl gave her sister a slow triumphant grin and then faded again without a sound.

No one moved for a long time after that, and no one spoke. And then, at last, the silence was broken by footsteps and voices in the hall outside. The door was flung open and Jessica looked up and saw her mother and Andrew. They were standing motionless in the doorway, staring into the room as though they couldn't believe their eyes.

9

"**W**ell, I'm *glad* we're going," Lizzie said, as she gazed out at the rain. "I never really liked this place, anyway. And after everything that's happened — "

"I know," Jessica said. "I hate this cottage too. I wish we'd never come here. It's all been a mistake." She looked across at Martin but he didn't say anything. Both boys were staring transfixed at the television set. On the screen, two cowboys were busily riding across a rocky hillside.

"That film looks familiar," Jessica said. "Isn't that the one you were watching last week, Liz?"

"Could be," Lizzie said. "They all look the same to me."

"If the fair one gets shot then it *is* the same film," Jessica said, and they all watched the television in silence, waiting to see what happened next. The two cowboys rode into a steep canyon and then one of the horses reared up and its rider fell to the ground with an arrow in his back.

"It's not the same film," Lizzie said. "There weren't any Red Indians in the one I saw."

"That's what I'd like to do to Beryl," Martin said.

"What?"

"Shoot her in the back with an arrow."

"There wouldn't be much point," Jessica said. "She's dead already, remember."

"I don't want to talk about Beryl," Lizzie said. "I want to forget we ever met her."

Jessica nodded, and turned back to the film. But she couldn't concentrate on the action on the screen; she kept remembering the terrible day of the tea party and how angry her mother had been when she and Andrew had seen the chaos in the sitting room. Luckily, the three old people had suffered no ill-effects from the experience but, as Martin had pointed out, they could easily have had heart attacks or worse. Andrew had taken them all home in the car, leaving Jessica's mother to supervise the cleaning-up operation and to tell the children exactly what she thought of them. Then, the next day, their parents had announced that they were cutting short the holiday and going back to London the day after that. There wasn't any point in staying on. Jessica's mother told the children grimly that they had ruined the holiday by their appalling behaviour and caused a great deal of extra expense into the bargain. The sitting room would have to be redecorated and a great deal of crockery needed to be replaced. Oddly enough, she added, Mrs Pengelly hadn't been as angry as she'd expected. It was almost as if she'd been prepared for something like this, as if it had happened before . . .

The door opened and Jessica looked up quickly. Her mother was standing in the doorway.

"Ah, there you all are," she said. "Andrew's just gone down to the village for some petrol and then we'll be on our way. I hope you've remembered to pack everything." No one answered, and she went on, "I'm just going next door to say goodbye to Mrs Pengelly. Though how I'll be able to look that woman in the face again, I don't know . . ." She disappeared, closing the door behind her. And then, almost immediately, it swung open again and a cold blast of air swept into the room.

"Shut the door, will you?" Martin said. "There's an awful draught in here."

"Shut it yourself," Jessica said automatically, and then her heart sank as she looked up and saw a shimmering shape in the air that could only mean one thing.

"Hullo," Beryl said timidly. "It's me again."

Jessica stared at her, not knowing what to say,

not knowing how to begin to express the rage she felt towards that thin-faced figure in the crumpled black gym-slip.

"I don't know how you have the nerve," she said at last. "I don't know how you *dare* show your face here after everything you've done."

"I know," Beryl said. "I've come to say I'm sorry."

Jessica hadn't expected this. "Sorry?" she said. "Yes, well, I expect you *are* sorry. But there's no excuse for the things you did. It was awful of you. I don't know how — "

"They asked for it," Beryl said sullenly. "Those ghastly old people asked for it, telling all those lies about me. None of the things they said were true. They were lying, all of them. I wasn't like that. I'm *not* like that, I'm *not* — "

"Oh, shut up and go away," Martin said wearily. "We don't care any more. We're leaving today and we'll never see you again. So none of it matters."

"Leaving?" Beryl's eyes widened with surprise. "Why are you leaving?"

"Because of your performance at the tea party," Martin said. "Why do you think?"

"But you *can't* go," Beryl said quickly. "We're just getting to know each other. I'm beginning to like you."

"You've a funny way of showing it," Lizzie told her.

"I won't do it again, I promise." Beryl's voice took on a pleading note. "Please stay. I *want* you to stay. We could have such fun together. We could — "

"It's too late," Jessica said coldly. "Our parents have decided that we're going and nothing *we* can say will change their minds. Anyway," she went on, staring straight into Beryl's imploring eyes, "we don't *want* to stay. We hate this place and we hate you. We never want to see you again as long as we live."

Beryl turned to Lizzie. "*You* don't feel like that, I know you don't," she said. "You'll stay, won't you? You're my friend. I like you better than any of the others. Tell them to stay. *Make* them stay. *Please!*" There was a tense silence then as Beryl gazed hopefully at Lizzie.

Then, "I don't want to stay either," Lizzie said defiantly. "I'll never forgive you for what you did. We were trying to be kind. We felt sorry for you. We thought you'd like to see your own brother and sisters. I'll never forgive you for spoiling it. Never." She turned away and stared out of the window.

Beryl looked at her for a moment and then turned back to the others, her eyes flashing with anger. "Well, go then," she snapped. "See if I care. I never really liked you, anyway. You're just like all the rest of them." Her voice sounded harsh and metallic again. She took a step towards Jessica. "Don't think you've seen the last of me yet," she hissed. "Because you haven't. Oh, no. You haven't seen the last of me." Then she faded swiftly away.

There was silence for a while after that, and then Martin cleared his throat and said briskly, "Well, that's the last we'll see of *her*, thank goodness. Come on, I think I can hear the car. Dad will be waiting for us." And he led the way out of the room.

Jessica stood at her bedroom window, gazing miserably down into the garden. Everything at home seemed just the same as ever but that was hardly surprising. They'd only been away for a few days and that was hardly any time at all. It felt as though they had never been away at all.

There was a knock at the door and Lizzie came in. "Isn't it *depressing*?" she said, flopping down on the bed.

"Better than being at the cottage, though," Jessica said.

"Oh, yes," Lizzie agreed. "Better than that. But I wish things had been, well, *different*."

"No rain."

"And no Monsters. Though they weren't too bad when we got to know them better. I'm glad they're staying with us here for a bit."

"And definitely no Beryl," Jessica said firmly.

"Oh, do shut up, Jess. I'm trying to forget all about her."

There was another knock on the door then, and their mother came in. "Can you spare a moment, you two?" she said. "I've just been unpacking one of the bags and I found this tucked at the bottom with the books and the swimming things. I've never seen it before. Does it belong to either of you?" Jessica saw she was holding in her hand a small black china cat.

The girls stared at the cat, and then Lizzie said, "I think it — it belongs to the cottage."

"Oh no!" her mother said. "How did it get in the bag then? We'll have to send it back."

"Yes, you'd better," Jessica said, exchanging a nervous glance with Lizzie. "I think you'd better send it back as soon as possible."

"Well then, *you* can do it," her mother snapped. "I imagine that you're responsible for taking it in the first place. So *you* can be responsible for sending it back to Mrs Pengelly. *With* a letter of apology." She put the cat on Jessica's dressing table and then stalked out of the room.

Jessica and Lizzie stared at the cat in silence for a moment. The little ornament seemed suddenly venomous, and Jessica shivered. "Are you thinking what I'm thinking?" she asked.

"I expect so," Lizzie whispered.

"We took the cat to the beach," Jessica said. "And she came too."

Lizzie's eyes were wide with fright. "You don't think — "

"Of course not," Jessica said briskly. She stood up and crossed to the dressing table. She looked at the black cat for a moment and then she opened a drawer and put the ornament inside. "There," she said. "Out of sight, out of mind. Come on, Liz. Let's go and find out what we're having for tea. I'm starving."

It was when they had finished tea and she was helping her mother to clear the table that Jessica glanced at the bulletin board by the washing machine. It was covered with a familiar jumble of picture postcards and scrawled messages and dentist's appointment cards and yellowing newspaper cuttings. But there was a small piece of paper in the bottom left-hand corner that she hadn't noticed before. She crossed to the board to take a closer look at it.

Jessica stared at the note for a moment or two. She couldn't make out the words at first, because the paper was creased and the writing was scratchy and uneven. But it didn't take her long to work out that it read:

BEWARE,
<u>THIS</u> HOUSE
IS HAUNTED
TOO!

APPLE®PACKS PAPERBACKS

Pick an Apple and Polish Off Some Great Reading!

NEW APPLE TITLES

☐ MT43356-3	**Family Picture** Dean Hughes	**$2.75**
☐ MT41682-0	**Dear Dad, Love Laurie** Susan Beth Pfeffer	**$2.75**
☐ MT41529-8	**My Sister, the Creep** Candice F. Ransom	**$2.75**

BESTSELLING APPLE TITLES

☐ MT42709-1	**Christina's Ghost** Betty Ren Wright	**$2.75**
☐ MT43461-6	**The Dollhouse Murders** Betty Ren Wright	**$2.75**
☐ MT42319-3	**The Friendship Pact** Susan Beth Pfeffer	**$2.75**
☐ MT43444-6	**Ghosts Beneath Our Feet** Betty Ren Wright	**$2.75**
☐ MT40605-1	**Help! I'm a Prisoner in the Library** Eth Clifford	**$2.50**
☐ MT42193-X	**Leah's Song** Eth Clifford	**$2.50**
☐ MT43618-X	**Me and Katie (The Pest)** Ann M. Martin	**$2.75**
☐ MT42883-7	**Sixth Grade Can Really Kill You** Barthe DeClements	**$2.75**
☐ MT40409-1	**Sixth Grade Secrets** Louis Sachar	**$2.75**
☐ MT42882-9	**Sixth Grade Sleepover** Eve Bunting	**$2.75**
☐ MT41732-0	**Too Many Murphys** Colleen O'Shaughnessy McKenna	**$2.75**
☐ MT41118-7	**Tough-Luck Karen** Johanna Hurwitz	**$2.50**
☐ MT42326-6	**Veronica the Show-off** Nancy K. Robinson	**$2.75**

Available wherever you buy books...or use the coupon below.

- -

Scholastic Inc., P.O. Box 7502, 2932 East McCarty Street, Jefferson City, MO 65102

Please send me the books I have checked above. I am enclosing $_____ (please add $2.00 to cover shipping and handling). Send check or money order — no cash or C.O.D. s please.

Name_____

Address_____

City _____ State/Zip _____

Please allow four to six weeks for delivery. Offer good in the U.S.A. only.
Sorry, mail orders are not available to residents of Canada. Prices subject to change.

APP1089

America's Favorite Series

THE BABY-SITTERS CLUB

by Ann M. Martin

Collect Them All!

The seven girls at Stoneybrook Middle School get into all kinds of adventures...with school, boys, and, of course, baby-sitting!